Draw some more aliens! Can you find the alien sticker?

How many robots can you find? Doodle some of your own!

How many robots can you find? Doodle some of your own!

Colour and decorate these naughty monsters!

Fill in the speech bubbles and doodle some funny faces!

How many boats can you find? Doodle some of your own!

How many planes can you find? Colour them in!

Help finish the drawings of these silly monsters! Create your own monster!

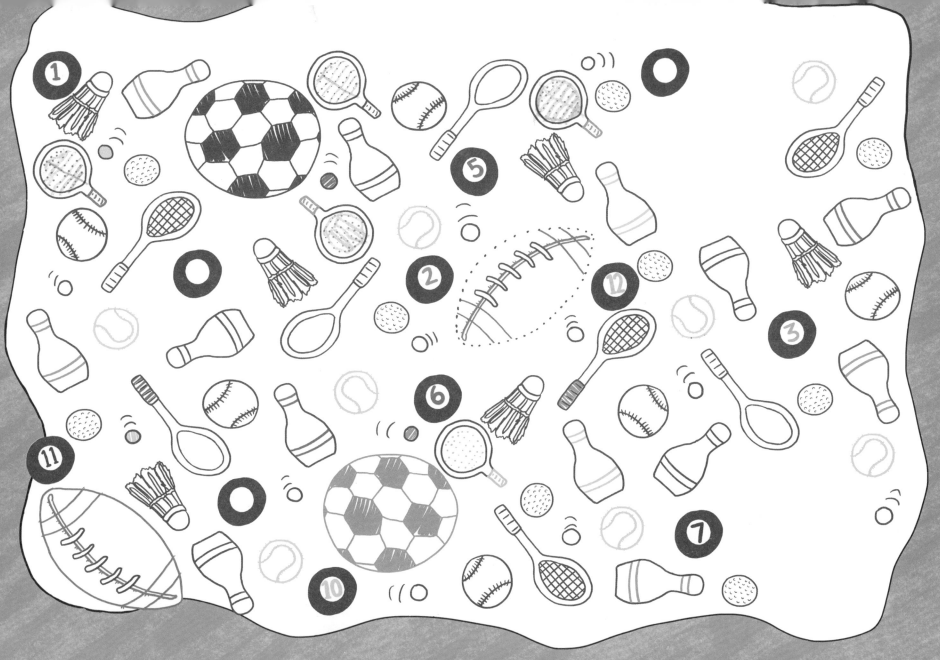

Colour and doodle your own sports equipment! Find the missing stickers!

Can you find the missing trainer sticker? Decorate the skateboards!

Colour and decorate these fiery dragons! Can you draw your own?

Help finish the drawings of these funny dinosaurs!

Can you find the missing robot sticker? How many robots can you count?

Can you find the stickers of the skulls? How many telescopes can you see?

Can you find the following: a screwdriver, 5 pairs of scissors, 7 bolts and a paintbrush sticker?

Colour in this jungle scene! Can you find the crown sticker for the lion?

Colour and decorate the turtles! Can you find the missing turtle sticker?

Fill the jar with yummy sweets! Can you find the missing sweet sticker?

Colour and decorate this space scene! Draw your own spaceship!

Can you find the missing kite sticker? Colour in the different kites!

Draw some more birds! Can you find the missing bird sticker?

Can you find the sticker of the trainers? Colour in your owns sports gear!

Can you find the star stickers? Join the dots on the two large stars!

Draw some faces on these silly monsters! Add your own monster in the frame!

Draw and colour in these fishy fish! Can you find the missing fish sticker?